A
WEE BIRD
WAS
WATCHING

A
Wee Bird
Was
Watching

KARINE POLWART

ILLUSTRATED BY

KATE LEIPER

Anna and her mum had been walking all day.

And the whole day before.

And the day before that.

It was a long time since they'd slept in their own beds.

They were sleepy and hungry and cold.

'Let's stop here and rest,' said Anna's mum. 'We can build a fire to keep warm.'

They peeled curls of bark for kindling, and stacked bracken, leaves and twigs into a pile.

A wee bird was watching.

Anna's mum took her firestone
from her pouch.

She struck it over and over
until a spark jumped
into the bark and leaves.

Anna blew gently
until the fire
caught hold.

Anna's mum pulled a blanket from her bag and tucked her daughter in beside the fire.

'I'm going to find us something to eat,' she whispered.

'Stay right here, Anna.'

Then she disappeared
into the trees.

The wood uttered strange sounds.
Whoops and whistles. Creaks and rustles.

Anna's mum plucked brambles from the bushes and dropped them into her bag.

Anna stared at the flickering fire until her eyes closed.

She didn't hear the **crinkling** of leaves, the **crunching** of twigs, as a wolf crept into the clearing.

But a wee bird was watching.

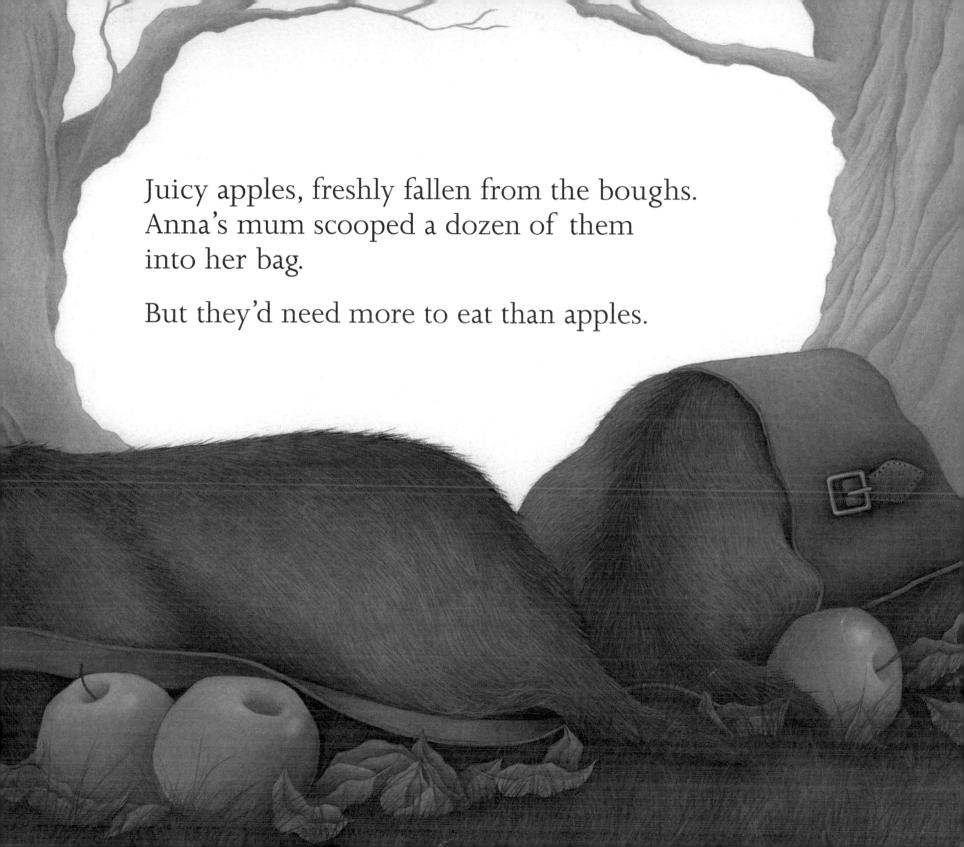

Juicy apples, freshly fallen from the boughs.
Anna's mum scooped a dozen of them
into her bag.

But they'd need more to eat than apples.

Snap. Crack. Snuffle.

The wolf crept in,
closer and closer.

Anna slept on.

The campfire beside her
grew smaller and weaker.

But a wee bird was watching.

Sweet chestnuts. Delicious,
roasted on the fire.

Anna's mum stuffed her
bag right up to the brim.

Now she had enough.

The fire was almost out.

Anna shuffled under the blanket.

The wolf took a deep breath
and got **ready to pounce** . . .

There was a **flash**, a **flutter**!

Down swooped the wee bird!

It was watching, and knew exactly what to do.

Just a wee grey bird –
tick, tick, ticking
in fury, as its claws
grazed the wolf.

The whirr of its wings
whipped up the dying fire.

Flames licked the wolf's face,
and it staggered back, yelping.

Anna woke with a cry
just in time to see the wee bird
tumble into the leaves.

The wolf scarpered back towards the trees,
as Anna's mum ran into the clearing.

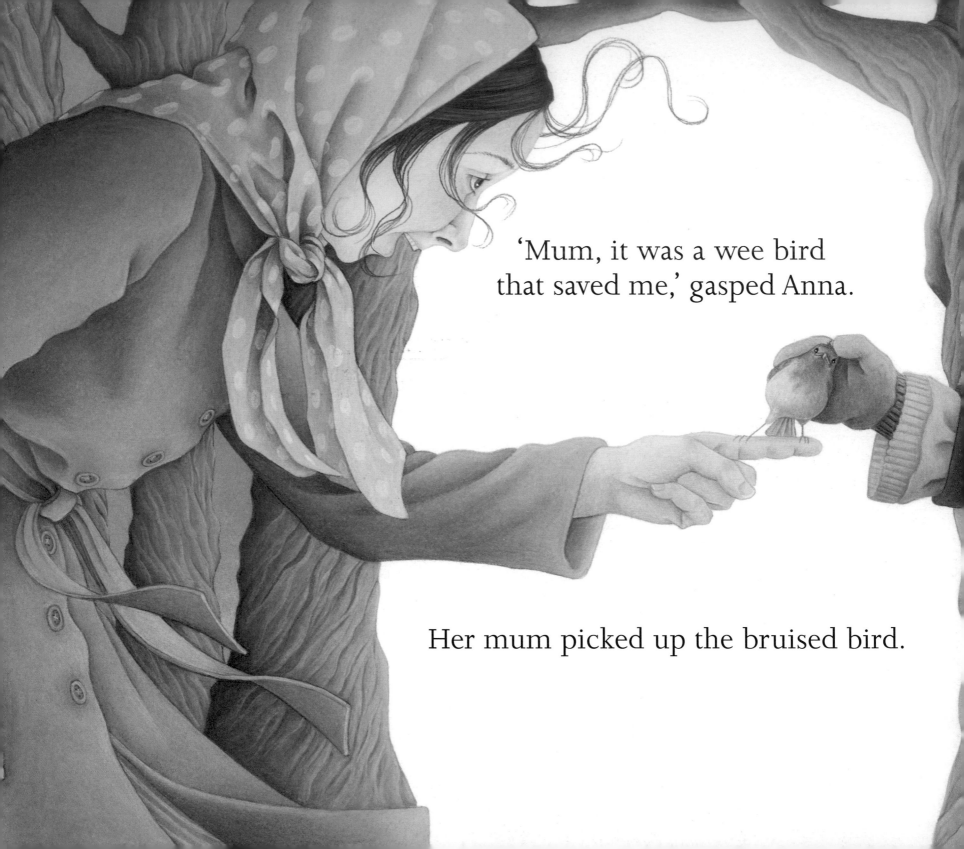

'Mum, it was a wee bird
that saved me,' gasped Anna.

Her mum picked up the bruised bird.

The brave wee thing!

The feathers on its breast
glowed a vibrant orange-red,
like the flames of the fire,
and its heart was thumping
like a tiny drum.

'Thank you, little Red Breast,'
Anna said.

All of this happened long ago, but that wee bird's feathers have glowed like fire ever since.

For this is the story of how the robin got its red breast.

With love to Arlo & Rosa, who know what to do. And to Anne, for the bramble jam (K.P.)

With love to Rayne, may wee birdies watch over you too (K.L.)

KARINE POLWART is a multi-award-winning Scottish songwriter and musician, as well as a theatre maker, storyteller, spoken-word performer and essayist. She is a six-times winner at the BBC Radio 2 Folk Awards. She lives by the woods and moors of Midlothian with her two children.

KATE LEIPER is an artist and illustrator who exhibits and undertakes commissions throughout the UK. She is drawn to mythical and animal subjects, and has previously worked on *An Illustrated Treasury of Scottish Folk and Fairy Tales*, *An Illustrated Treasury of Scottish Mythical Creatures* and *The Book of the Howlat*.

First published in 2018
by BC Books, an imprint of Birlinn Limited
West Newington House, 10 Newington Road
Edinburgh EH9 1QS

www.bcbooksforkids.co.uk

ISBN 978 178027 532 1

British Library Cataloguing-in-Publication Data
A catalogue record for this book is available from the British Library

Designed by James Hutcheson and typeset in Monotype Johanna
Printed and bound by Latimer Trend, Plymouth.